WITHDRAWN

D

NC

D

THE EGG TREE

STORY AND PICTURES
BY

KATHERINE MILHOUS

CHARLES SCRIBNER'S SONS, NEW YORK

ACKNOWLEDGMENTS

TO CARRIE MAY UMBERGER PALSGROVE
who, many years ago, made a little Easter Egg Tree for her own children. Each year since, the tree has grown larger and larger. Last year's tree had fourteen hundred eggs hanging on its branches and was shown in the Historical Society of Berks County, Pennsylvania.

TO HATTIE AND ANNA LA ROSS GROSS
of Quakertown, Pennsylvania, whose artist grandfather painted the original eggs from which the traditional egg designs in this book are taken.

TO FRANCES LICHTEN
author of "Folk Art of Rural Pennsylvania". Many decorative motifs from this treasury of folk art appear in the border designs and elsewhere in this book.

TO THE PEOPLE OF THE RED HILLS
known as the Pennsylvania Dutch, who love bold color and designs, and who hold fast to their traditions which are rooted in far away times and in far off lands.

It was very early on Easter morning. So early that the children were still asleep in the small red house and the animals were quiet in the big red barn. All except the rooster.

Suddenly the rooster threw out his chest as if he were blowing a horn.

"Cock-a-doodle-doo! This will never do!" he crowed. Just then the sun came up over the Red Hills. The rooster crowed again and all the animals woke up. The third time he crowed he woke up Katy and Katy woke up Carl.

"Carl! Get up! Maybe we can see the Easter Rabbit bring the eggs."

Katy and Carl tiptoed across the floor to the window and flung open the shutters. How good the outdoors smelled! And how lovely the garden looked!

"The Rabbit hasn't come yet!" said Katy. "See, there are the flower petals I put for him on the lawn. He hasn't eaten a one."

Carl laughed. "I don't believe the Easter Rabbit

eats flower petals. If you want the Rabbit to come you have to whistle for him. Like this.....”

“S-sh,” said Katy. “Grandmom said we mustn’t wake up our cousins till it’s time for the egg hunt.”

“But there won’t be any egg hunt if the Rabbit doesn’t bring the eggs,” said Carl. He whistled again, a bit louder. He hoped his cousins in the next bedroom would hear him and get up. Then they, too, could see the Rabbit bring the eggs.

Carl and Katy leaned out the window. The morning was full of sounds. Birds twittered, cows mooed, horses neighed, pigs grunted, geese honked and hens cackled. Church bells rang out from the village over the hill. But still the Easter Rabbit did not come. Once there was a rustle under the big lilac bush—but it was only the cat.

“Whistle just once more, please, Carl,” Katy said.

This time Carl whistled with all his might. Suddenly Katy put her hand over his mouth.

“S-sh, Carl. There’s the Rabbit! In the garden! And he’s nibbling the flower petals.”

The children held their breaths. How the Rabbit bounced about the flower beds and burrowed in the bushes! At last he bounded out of sight behind the barn.

"Come on, Katy!" said Carl. "Let's wake everybody up." He ran down the hall, calling: "Sus-y! Luk-ey! John-ny! Appo-lonia! The Easter Rabbit has come."

In a few minutes all the children were dressed and out in the barnyard. The egg hunt had begun. Grandmom smiled from the kitchen door. Which child would win the prize for finding the most eggs? It would not be Carl or Katy, she was sure, for this was their first egg hunt. The other grandchildren had come every Easter to the little red house.

At first Katy and Carl thought hunting for colored eggs the greatest fun in the world. But somehow their cousins found all the pretty eggs. Katy and Carl just did not know where to look. Who would think that the Rabbit had left eggs in the feed bin, in the watering trough, and even up in the hayloft?

In the garden it was even harder—the colored

eggs looked so much like the colored flowers. But at last Carl found a nest of three eggs in a magnolia tree. Now Katy was the only one who had not found a single egg.

In the kitchen the egg hunt began all over again. Katy was sure she would find eggs in the kitchen. But here, too, the Rabbit had left eggs in the strangest places—in the clock case, in the cookie cutters, and even under the butter churn.

Katy began to run round and round like a waltzing mouse. If only she could find just one egg! Even little Appolonia had found an egg and was already eating it.

"Hurray! I found another egg!" shouted Carl, running out of the stair closet. "I have the most!"

"No, I have," said Luke. He lifted a purple egg from the teapot. "I have five!"

Round and round the kitchen ran Katy but now she wanted only to run away and hide. She felt so stupid. Just then she saw the attic stairs. Maybe the Easter Rabbit had left eggs for her in the attic. Katy began to climb the creaking stairs.

The big attic was dark and lonely. Katy shivered a little. Soon it did not seem quite so dark and she could see into the far corners. A spider was busy spinning her silken web across a bar of sunlight.

What was that on the shelf in the dark corner? A box? It looked like a hat box. Katy tiptoed across the dusty floor. Could the Easter Rabbit have left eggs in an old hat box? No, of course not. How silly she was!

She climbed up on a chest and lifted the lid of the hat box. And there were eggs—all packed snugly in an old beaver hat! It must have been a long time since someone had put them away. Katy took out the eggs carefully. One—two—three—four—five—six.

What beautiful colors! And there were pictures on the eggs. Katy took the hatful of eggs and walked slowly down the stairs. The Easter Rabbit had not forgotten her, after all. She was sure that she had won the prize.

But there was Carl in the kitchen with a whole

pile of eggs on the table. He was very excited.

"I've found TWELVE eggs! I've won! I've won!"

"I found—six," Katy said, and put her hatful on the table beside Carl's.

Grandmom stopped laying the breakfast cloth. Her eyes grew big and round.

"Why, I'd forgotten all about those eggs! I'm glad you found them, Katy. And now for the prize. Carl has the prize for the most eggs, but Katy has won the prize for the most beautiful eggs."

Grandmom gave them each a big cookie rabbit with an egg baked in its middle.

Now it was breakfast time. The children began to crack and eat the eggs they had found in the egg hunt. Grandmom brought a big pitcher of milk and Katy and Carl shared their cookie rabbits with the other children.

"Let's eat the eggs Katy found in the attic," said little Appolonia who was still hungry.

"No—No—No—NO—NO!" said Grandmom. "The very idea! Besides, they're all hollow inside."

Grandmom sat down, holding the eggs in her lap.
"I painted these eggs myself when I was a young
girl. Right here in this kitchen I painted them. They
turned out so pretty that I kept them all these years.
But now each of you may choose one for your own,
to keep always."

Carl chose first. He picked out an egg with a picture of a fine galloping horse on it. Katy chose an egg with a lovely bird sitting on a branch.

Katy held up her egg and looked at it closely. She turned it round and round to see all the bright colors.

Susy, Luke and Johnny each chose an egg. Now there was only one egg left in the old hat.

"Why, this egg has the letter A on it!" said Grandmom. "A is for Appolonia."

Appolonia took the egg. "It's pretty," she said. "But I do wish it was good to eat."

The children put their eggs in a row on the window seat. "Now, what shall we do with them?" they asked.

"We don't do anything with them," said Katy. "They are so beautiful, we just LOOK at them."

Grandmom did not say a word. She put on her shawl and went out the kitchen door. In a few minutes she came back carrying a small tree. She fixed the tree so that it would stand on the table. Then she ran a thread through each of the beautiful eggs and hung them on the tree.

"Why, it's an Easter Egg Tree!" said Katy.

"An Easter Egg Tree! An Easter Egg Tree!" sang the children, dancing around the tree.

It was a lovely tree, but it was so very small.

Suddenly Carl stood still. "Grandmom," he said, "please show us how to make eggs with pictures on them. Then we can have a bigger tree."

"Why, certainly," said Grandmom. "First thing tomorrow morning. Today we keep Easter."

The next morning when the children came down stairs they found Grandmom dyeing eggs in the kettles over the fireplace. They hurried through breakfast for they could scarcely wait to learn how to make pictures on the gay colored eggs.

There were not enough paints to go round, so Grandmom said the boys would have to scratch designs on the eggs with their pocket knives. Grandmom took sheets of paper and drew all the designs she could remember. Each picture had a name—The Bright and Morning Star, The Deer on the Mountain, The Cooing Dove, The Pomegranate, The Horn-blowing Rooster.

"Oh, Grandmom, paint an egg with the Horn-blowing Rooster!" the children begged. So Grandmom painted a handsome rooster blowing a horn.

All the children found they could make pictures on the eggs. Even little Appolonia could paint The Bright and Morning Star. Soon the table was gay as a flower garden with all the painted eggs.

Now they had enough eggs to make a big tree.

"Let's go and find one—right away," said Carl.

Carl and Luke and Johnny went to the woods and they came back with a young white birch tree. It was so large that it had to stand on the floor. The children trimmed the tree with the eggs they had painted themselves and with many plain dyed ones. Susy and Appolonia hung small baskets from the branches. Under the tree Grandmom placed an enormous cookie rabbit which she had just taken from the oven.

Katy hung up the eggs she had found in the attic. If she had not found those eggs they would never have had an Egg Tree, Grandmom said. Katy felt very proud as she hung her egg with the lovely bird on the topmost branch.

"It is such a beautiful tree!" said Katy. "I wish that everyone in the world could see it."

"Yes," said Grandmom. "It makes a body feel as if Spring has come right into the house. We must give a party for it."

So Grandmom gave a party for the tree. All the children from all the farms about were invited.

"An Egg Tree!" they said. "We've never seen a tree that grows eggs on its branches!"

The children went home and told their fathers and mothers about it. The fathers and mothers all came to see the wonderful tree in the little red house.

"Next Easter we'll have a bigger tree," Katy said.

"A really big tree," said Carl.

Next year the children began weeks ahead of Easter to trim the Egg Tree. This time the tree was so tall that its top touched the ceiling. Hundreds of eggs hung from its branches. When the sun streamed in the tree looked like a piece of the rainbow. More than ever Katy wished that everyone in the world could see their lovely tree.

"Land's sakes!" said Grandmom, who was standing by the window. "Who are all those people coming up the driveway?"

They were village people who had heard about the wonderful Egg Tree. More people came to see the tree, and more and more and more. They came from near and they came from far. Some even came from the big city. The little red house had become famous.

Children brought presents to put under the tree— Easter toys and bright baskets and painted wooden eggs from lands across the sea.

"Thank you very much for letting us see the tree,"

the visitors said. "And now we are going home and make our own Easter Egg Tree."

Grandmom looked very pleased. "That's just fine!" she said. "There's nothing like an Easter Egg Tree to bring Spring into the house. A happy Easter to you all!"

When all the visitors had gone the little red house seemed very quiet. The children sat on the floor and played with the presents spread out under the tree. Suddenly Katy ran up to Grandmom and hugged her.

"Oh, Grandmom!" she said. "Everybody in the world really did come to see our Egg Tree, didn't they?"

Grandmom laughed. "A body would think so to look at this floor," she said. Then she took up her broom and began to sweep briskly. Tomorrow would be Easter and the house must be fresh and clean.

Katy ran out of doors and picked some flowers in the garden. She scattered the bright-colored petals on the lawn for the Easter Rabbit's breakfast. It would never do to forget the Easter Rabbit, for the Easter Rabbit had not forgotten her.

THE END